Happy Easter
Adam

Love
Granmommy
Grandaddy

APRIL 3, 1994

White NINETEENS

DAVID CHRISTIANA

Farrar · Straus · Giroux
New York

"Such a beautiful morning deserves my most beautiful wings," said Buttercup as she got out of bed. But when she opened the wooden box, her favorite wings were gone. "Who took my White Nineteens, and why?"

Buttercup asked the Owl
if he had seen someone
steal a pair of wings
during the night.

"Twooo blue eyes, but
whooo knows whose?"
yawned the Owl, and he
went back to sleep.

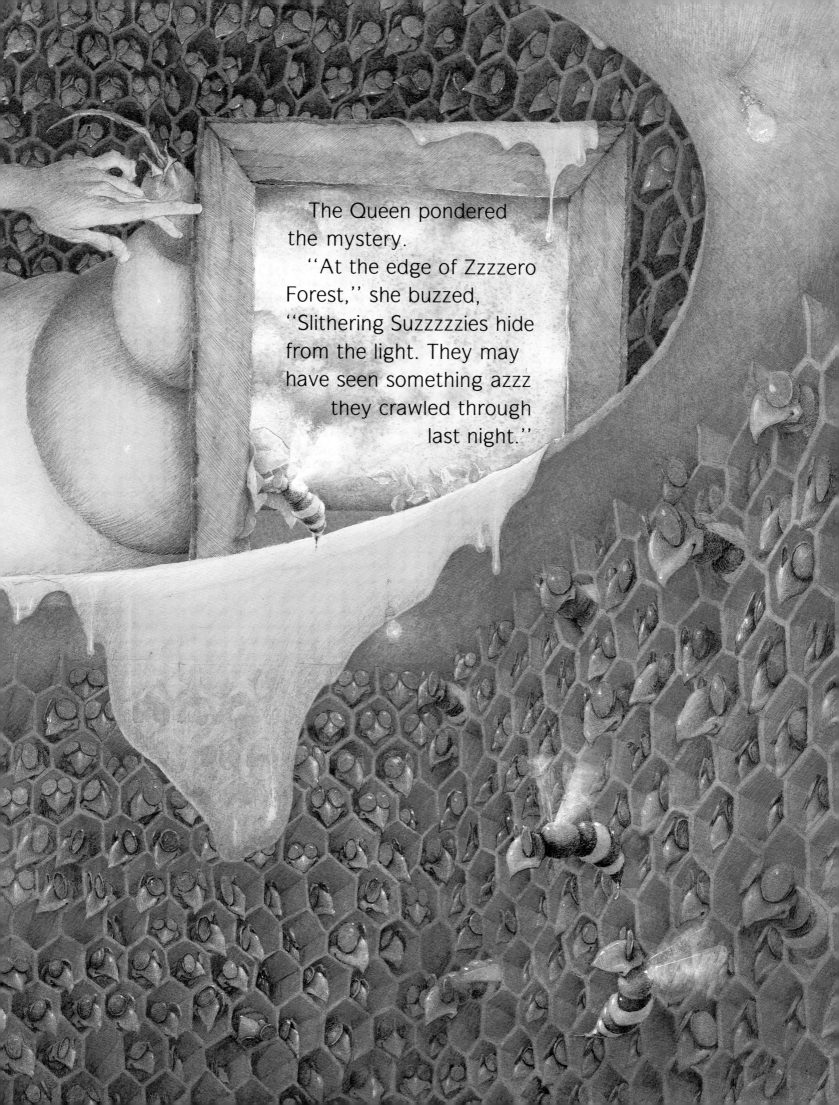

The Queen pondered the mystery.

"At the edge of Zzzzero Forest," she buzzed, "Slithering Suzzzzzies hide from the light. They may have seen something azzz they crawled through last night."

At dusk, Buttercup and
her escorts met a slew of
Slithering Suzzies as they
inched out of the ground.
   "Wasn't me," drawled one.
   "Wasn't us," drawled
the others. "Did y'all try the
Opposite Side of the Forest?
Or are you afraid of . . ."

The Cat ran away with
stingers in his ears. Could
he have been the thief?
"He does *act* like one,"
thought Buttercup.
She followed him through
to the Opposite Side.

POSITE SIDE

"But why would the Cat
take my White Nineteens?''
His tracks led her to
a curious, rusty lump in
the snow.

When she peered inside, there was the Cat curled up with a Troll. And on the Troll's hairless head ...her White Nineteens.

"My toes are by the fire," he said. "My ears are warm as stew. I bet when Mrs. Troll gets home, she'll want some ear wings, too."

Two blue eyes had spied
a flutter of pink and
the Cat bolted out into
the snow. Without delay,
he returned to the Troll
with Buttercup in hand.

"Give that thing with wings to me," said the Troll. "I'll tie them up together. Save 'em for my Mrs. Troll. 'Cause no ears like cold weather."

It was time for the Troll and the Cat to settle down and take their nap.

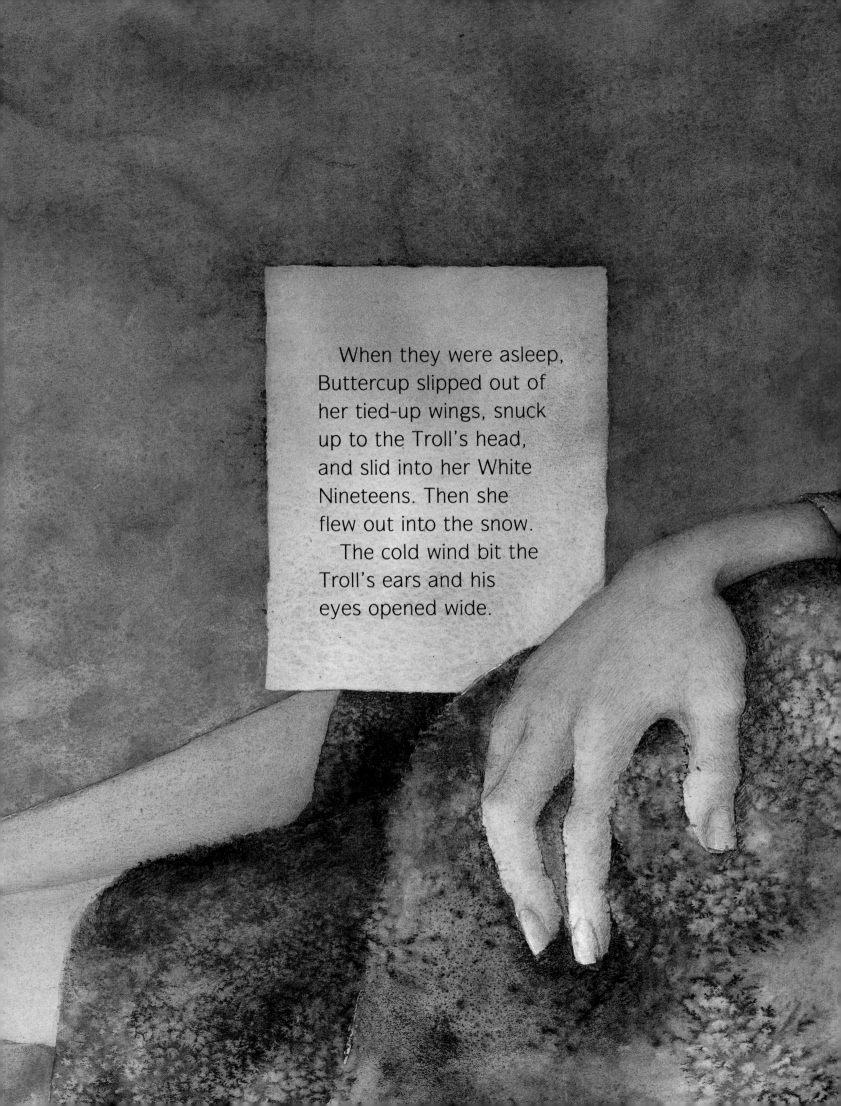

When they were asleep,
Buttercup slipped out of
her tied-up wings, snuck
up to the Troll's head,
and slid into her White
Nineteens. Then she
flew out into the snow.
The cold wind bit the
Troll's ears and his
eyes opened wide.

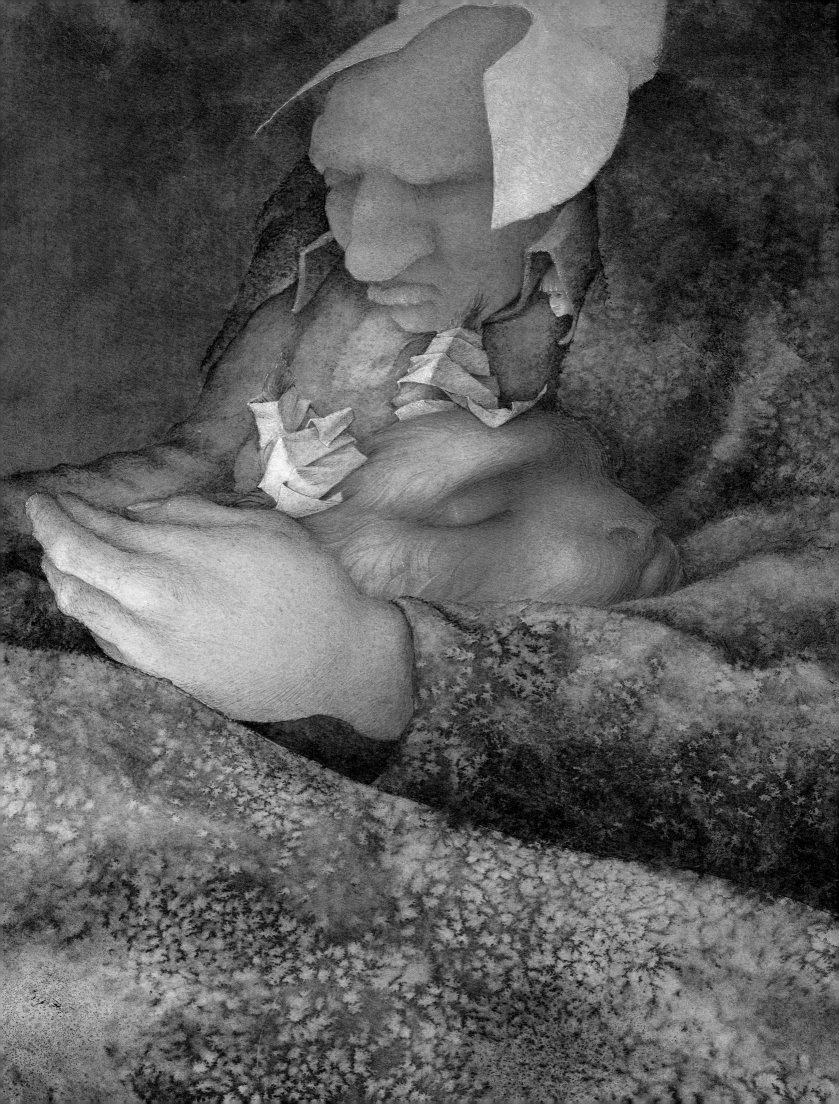

So he and the Cat went white-wing hunting until the sun went down. They were very late for supper.

"Hope Mrs. Troll ain't mad," thought the Cat. "Where'd those pink things go?"

The Troll and the
Cat shuffled home and
Buttercup flew back
into another summer
morning in the Forest…

. . . while Mrs. Troll
danced in her new
pink ear wings.